FSC
www.fsc.org
MIX
Paper from
responsible sources
FSC® C043106

Snow Bears Never Lie

A story by SAID
Illustrated by Marine Ludin

North
South

"I'm going to pick some berries," said Lily.

"Make sure you come home before dark," said her mother, tying a scarf round her neck.

"Ye-ye-yeeeees!" sang Lily, picking up a basket and dancing out the door.

She climbed up the hill to her family's best berry patch.

"Oh, what's this? An icebox in the middle of the forest?
And who's sitting in it, all squashed up? A bear!"
"Shut the door, girl!" grumbled the bear.
"My name's Lily, not 'girl,'" said Lily very firmly.

"Well, I'm Snow Bear," said the bear. He was huge and white, with a thick fur coat.

"So who squeezed you into the icebox?" asked Lily.

"Nobody," said the bear.

"Then why were you in there?"

"Because . . . because it's too warm out here."

"Too warm?" cried Lily, who was shivering with the cold.

"You don't know much about snow bears, do you? I need lots of snow and ice."

Lily scratched the back of her head and thought things over.
"What do snow bears like to eat?" she asked.

"When I'm at home, I feed on berries. I pick them, then I lie down in the snow, put them all over my stomach, and throw them one by one into my mouth."

"Then why have you come here?" asked Lily after a few moments.

"Well, I was looking for something to eat in the snow, and wandered too far away from home."

"So what are you going to do now?"
"I'm waiting for the wind and then
I'll fly with it back to the North Pole.
It's nice and cold there."
"You can fly?" cried Lily.

"Of course I can fly. All snow bears can fly."

"On your own, just like that?" asked Lily in disbelief.

"Well, no, not on my own just like that."

"What else do you need?"

"Without the wind I can't fly an inch."

"When is the wind coming, then?"

"When night begins to fall." The snow bear looked up at the sky. "Ah, it'll be dark soon."

"Yes, it will," said Lily a little anxiously. "And I still haven't picked any berries."

"I'll see to the berries," said the bear, "and I can also make two more of your wishes come true."

"Just like that?" asked Lily.

"It's a reward for waking me—otherwise I'd have missed the wind."

"I'd like to fly, and I'd like not to be afraid of the dark," said Lily at once.

"No problem," said the snow bear. He took Lily's hand, whirled her three times around his head, and threw her with a mighty heave high in the air.

"Hurray! I can fly!" shouted Lily.
"But I had another wish too . . .
about the dark, remember?"

"Climb up on my back and hold tight to my fur!" shouted the bear.
He ran deep into the dark forest. Then he set Lily down on the
ground. "Are you still afraid of the dark?" he asked.
"No."
"Why not?"
"Because you're here," she said, cuddling up to the bear.
"And supposing you were alone?" he asked.
"I'd be afraid."
"Then all you have to do is close your eyes and think of me."
"Then I won't be afraid?" asked Lily.
"Guaranteed," said the bear.
"Well, I don't know . . . ," mumbled Lily.
"Snow bears never lie."
"In that case, I believe you."

"There you are, then," said the bear. "I think I should take you home now."

Lily jumped up on the bear's back.

"I like your soft white fur," she said.

"And I like your soft red scarf," said the bear.

"Then you can have it as a reward for giving me a ride."

"Thank you," said the bear. "Are we ready?"

"We're ready!" cried Lily. "Giddyup!"

Lily was so tired that she soon fell fast asleep.

The bear picked some berries and then carried Lily all the way home. He knocked three times on the front door, and gave the sleeping Lily a goodbye kiss on the cheek.

He was just about to leave, but first he bent down and picked up her scarf.

"Now I shall always remember you," he said, and hurried away.

Lily's father carried her into the house.
Now Lily woke up.
"Where have you been all this time?" asked her mother.

Lily rubbed her eyes and saw the basketful of berries on her mother's arm.

"I was in the forest with a snow bear," said Lily proudly.

"With who?" asked her father.

"With a snow bear," answered Lily. Then she clapped her hands and cried, "Now I can fly, and I'm not afraid of the dark anymore."

"So our Lily's not afraid of the dark anymore!" said her father.

"And she can fly," said her mother. "But where's your scarf?"

"Oh, I gave it to the snow bear as a souvenir."

"Aha, I see, as a souvenir," said her mother.

"But in exchange he's taught her to fly!" said her father.

"That's right, I can fly!"

"On your own, just like that?" asked her mother.

"Well, no, not on my own just like that."

"What else do you need?"

"Without the snow bear I can't fly an inch."

Then Lily reached into the basket, took out some berries, put them all over her stomach, threw them one by one into her mouth, and smiled a great big smile.